Charlotte Zolotow

The Park Book

Pictures by H. A. Rey

A Harper Trophy Book

Harper & Row, Publishers

*For **MAURICE***

(a former boy)

The Park Book
Copyright 1944 by Harper & Row, Publishers, Inc.
Text copyright renewed 1972 by Charlotte Zolotow
Illustrations copyright renewed 1972 by H. A. Rey
Printed in the U.S.A. All rights reserved.
Library of Congress Catalog Card Number: 44–9471
ISBN 0-06-026970-7 (lib. bdg.)
ISBN 0-06-443092-8 (pbk.)
First Harper Trophy edition, 1986.

WHAT is the park like?" asked a little boy

who lived in the country and played all day

in the wide meadow beside his house.

And his mother told him.

In the very early morning when the light is pale gold the park cleaner comes with his long pointed pole. He spears the things of yesterday, the ice-cream wrappers, the cigarette butts, the pink paper from chewing gum, and peanut shells the wind has blown across the grass.

Mr. Humphrey Gillingwater, reading

his paper as he walks along, doesn't see

the park cleaner. Neither does Selma Daley

in her new summer hat. For like the other

hurrying people they rush to get to

work on time.

The shoeshine man

rubs his hands together

looking at the people's feet as they hurry past.

"Shiinnnnnnne?" he calls. "Shinnemmmmmmup?"

But no one stops so early.

Baby-sitters and grandmothers and young mothers come

joggling carriages before them. Soft little babies look out with

wonder at boys and girls big enough to scuff along beside the carriages.

The sunlight dances in the branches of the trees and reaches down to

the low-looped iron fence that holds the green grass in.

The people settle on the benches.

The sun is warmer now.

A little boy who had pancakes for breakfast

and a little girl who ate bread and jam

play together in the sand pile.

A little boy who goes to bed at seven and a little girl

who is allowed to stay up till seven-thirty seesaw up and down.

A little girl who has no brothers or sisters and

a little boy who has two sisters and a brother take turns at the swing.

A shy little girl watches a pigeon pecking

and strutting across the sidewalk. She

waves her arms at him and the pigeon

goes a few clawsteps away, then blows

up his feathers and struts back past the

little girl to another pigeon who is waiting

on the grass. A little way away on a bench to himself is

an old man with a bag of bread crumbs. As he scatters each handful the pigeons ripple up to his feet

in a blue and silver wave. A very

small boy stands there as still as a

small stone statue, only his eyes are

shining. When the old man looks up

at him he suddenly turns and runs off

to bury his head in his mother's

lap. That's how small he is!

A shiny black cocker spaniel dozes under a bench
across the way. The sun gets higher and higher
until the whole park is shining. The old man
uses up his crumbs, crumples his brown paper bag
and gets up. Leaning ahead of each step he
shuffles away. The mothers look up
at the sun as their hungry babies
wake for lunch. And the little
children all come out of
the playground

and take their mothers' hands to go home.

Now the park belongs to the birds for a little while.

They twitter at each other from the branches of the

trees. Only the shoeshine man sees them as they

hop from branch to branch giving

the tree a little shake each time.

When the shoeshine man goes to take a drink he startles three small sparrows out of the water fountain. The sun shines hot and strong now in the park. It climbs up the curved metal legs of the benches and makes them gleam like gold.

The afternoon begins. The bumbling carriages come again, little children shouting with pleasure, bigger children sailing past on their bikes.

A baseball game begins. First there is the thunk of the bat, then the curve of the ball in the air and the thick smack as it lands in the catcher's glove.

"Shinemmmmmmmmup!" calls the shoeshine man. "Shoes, shinemmmmmmmmmup."

Tinkinkinkle goes the ice-cream man's cart. "Bal-loons," calls the balloon man, "BAL-loons." The park is loud with light and sound. You can hardly hear the birds. A squirrel with a bushy tail races halfway down a tree trunk and stops, spraddled, as though he had grown out of it. Then he leaps to the grass, hops, pauses, hops, until he has crossed

the sidewalk to

where the people sit. He stands up on his hind legs, holding his little

paws against his heart, and swishes his big tail nervously as he begs for nuts.

Just so three little boys stand watching the ice-cream man recite his flavors

to a little girl who can't decide.

A little white boat sets sail in the rough waters

of the fountain and capsizes.

The captain pulls it out by the string and sets

it sailing again.

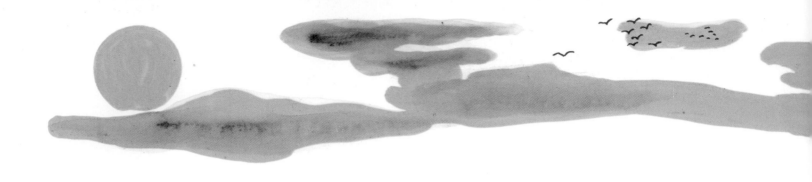

The sun begins to go down. The carriages, the big and small

children, start now one by one until they are all streaming out

of the park toward home.

The sky is purple and the reflection of the sun glows in the

windows of the buildings around the park. It looks as though

there were a warm fire shining from every home.

The people who hurried through the park in the morning come

home in the purple light.

Mr. Humphrey Gillingwater tucks his glasses
in his pocket, clasps the paper behind his back
and looks up at the evening sky. Selma Daley
pulls off her hat and lets the soft park wind
run through her hair.

Already the orange light is fading from the windows. Gray shadows cover the trees and sidewalks and buildings around the park. The footsteps are nearly gone and there is only the lonely song of one late bird going from branch to branch toward his nest. Even the shoeshine man picks up his box and goes home.

The lights in the homes of the people who have just left the park begin to go on. The bright windows shine in the dark sky around the park. And when the park lights go on they look like a chain of round golden balls hung in the trees. The park is still. Behind the lighted windows people eat their dinners and the little children who played so hard in the park take their baths and go to bed.

As the lights in the children's rooms go out, the park begins another life.

Boys and girls who have grown up walk slowly along the dark paths holding

hands. The air is cool and moist with the smell of grass. The squirrels

are in their tree trunks, the shoeshine man is gone. Only the water fountain

goes on as it did in the day. But it is strange and beautiful in the white

moonlight.

The grown-up boys and girls sit on the benches whispering to each other.

Some of them talk about the ships they will sail, the books they will write,

the music they want to play. One by one now the lights in the windows

of the mothers and fathers go out.

The trees and benches and grass look silver in the moonlight. And at last when the moon is high, the grown-up boys and girls know they too must go, and start homeward hand in hand.

They pass all the city dogs out for their evening run in the park—a little

dachshund rocking from side to side on his short legs, and a little black-

and-tan twinkling along the end of his lead like a ballet dancer. Round and

round in a wide moonlit stretch of grass two Irish setters race, barking into

the nighttime stillness of

the park. A little black scotty and a big brown boxer play tug-a-leash. A

little white dog lies on her back in the grass, wiggles and rubs, waving all

four paws happily in the air. Then as their owners call, the dogs return,

cold-nosed and breathless, to their people who lead them out of the park

to their homes.

Now the lights in the buildings around the park are all out.

Only the starry sky surrounds the park. All the people who belong

to its waking hours are gone. On one bench an old man who has

no darkened window to sleep behind covers himself with newspapers

and listens to the soft wind sighing in the trees.

The moon is very high in the sky.

There are no sounds in the park now,

except the echo of the milk carts rattling over the cobblestones

of a near-by street. Everyone is asleep. The city is dark. The park

is dark and waiting.

For soon a new day will begin.

"It doesn't have all the things a meadow has,"

said the little boy, "but I like the park."

The End

"Legend has it that [when] **Charlotte Zolotow,** then Ursula Nordstrom's secretary, suggested a park book as an antidote to visions of rural bliss...she was told to 'write it.'" (*American Picturebooks from Noah's Ark to the Beast Within* by Barbara Bader, Macmillan, 1976)

And so she did, creating a classic. Ms. Zolotow has written more than sixty picture books since then, including MR. RABBIT AND THE LOVELY PRESENT, illustrated by Maurice Sendak; and the groundbreaking WILLIAM'S DOLL and the timeless MY GRANDSON LEW, both illustrated by William Pène du Bois. Ms. Zolotow lives in Hastings-on-Hudson, New York.

H. A. Rey is the illustrator of the beloved CURIOUS GEORGE stories, written together with his wife, Margret Rey. The books have been translated into numerous languages and have sold more than 20 million copies throughout the world. He and Ms. Rey also collaborated on PRETZEL and PRETZEL'S PUPPIES. Mr. Rey wrote and illustrated many other books for adults and children, among them the recently revised and reissued standard FIND THE CONSTELLATIONS. Mr. Rey died in 1977.